The Hero of Barletta

Carolrhoda Books · Minneapolis, Minnesota

The Hero of Barletta

by **Donna Jo Napoli**
illustrated by **Dana Gustafson**

To my family

Library of Congress Cataloging-in-Publication Data

Napoli, Donna Jo, 1948-
  The hero of Barletta.

  (Carolrhoda on my own books)
  Summary: A clever giant saves the town of Barletta from an advancing army. [1. Folklore — Italy] I. Gustafson, Dana, ill. II. Title. III. Series: Carolrhoda on my own book.
  PZ8.1.N24He 1988   398.2′1 [E]   87-20837
  ISBN 0-87614-277-3 (lib. bdg.)

Manufactured in the United States of America

1 2 3 4 5 6 7 8 9 10 98 97 96 95 94 93 92 91 90 89 88

A long time ago,
in a town called Barletta,
there lived a boy named Nico.
Nico was a child,
but he was just as big
as most grown-ups.

5

When the other children
played hide-and-seek,
they did not ask Nico.
"You're too big," said Roberto.
"You always stick out."

When the other children ran races,
they did not ask Nico.
"Your legs are too long," said Silvio.
"You always win."

And when the other children
played ball, they did not ask Nico.
"You throw too hard," said Enrico.
"We can't catch your balls."

Often Nico sat by himself
and watched the children
play their games.
He still hoped that someone
would ask him to join in,
but no one ever did.
Finally Nico would walk away
and play with his dog, Nero, instead.

In time, the children grew older
and began to work.
Roberto learned to make shoes.
Silvio learned to blow glass.
Enrico learned to bake bread.

Nico watched the other boys work.

He wanted to work too.

He wanted to help his father
build fireplaces.

But he had grown too big
to work indoors.

Soon Nico was as tall
as a young pine tree.

He had to sleep outside in a hammock
that his father made for him.

His mother put a table in the courtyard
so the family could eat together.

Nico's mother saw
how unhappy he was.
She said, "Nico, my dear boy,

14

why don't you work
in the fields outside the town walls?
You are strong.
You would be a help to the farmers."

So in the spring, Nico went out
to the fields.
He plowed and he planted.
At lunchtime he ran with Nero
among the apricot trees.
He peeked in the birds' nests.
He whistled with the birds
when they sang.
The birds were Nico's friends.
They saw the world from above,
just as he did.

Soon the days got hot and long,
and the people of Barletta
had their summer festival.
Young men in costumes carried flags
and raced on horses.

After the race, the younger boys
lined up for rides on the winning horse.
Nico lined up too,
but the horse's owner stopped him.
"Nico, why don't YOU give
my HORSE a ride, instead?"
Everyone laughed.

Nico ran back outside the town walls.
He could still hear the laughter
of the townspeople in his ears.
He whistled to Nero.
They went swimming together
in the large river north of town.
Then they sat on the bridge in the sun.

In autumn,

when the nights became chilly,

Nico could not

sleep outside anymore.

He had to sleep in the church.

It was the only building

big enough for him.

Winter came.

Nico could no longer work
in the frozen fields.

He missed the birds.

He wished that he had friends
he could talk to.

But Nico was so big now that no one
in Barletta could talk to him easily.

He often felt lonely.

Nico's father showed him how
to carve a wooden flute.

Nico played his flute to Nero
as they waited for spring.

Finally it was warm.

The farmers planted their crops.

Nico went back to work in the fields.

He cared for the plum trees
in the orchard.

One day,
while Nico was working in the orchard,
he saw a man run over the bridge.

Nico followed him.

The man ran into the town square
shouting, "The enemy is coming!
They have captured
all the northern towns!
Arm yourselves!
Get ready for war!"

The townspeople went wild with fear.
"Who here has seen the enemy?"
shouted the mayor.
"What do they look like?"
No one knew,
but everyone wanted to guess.
"They have long teeth like wolves!"
"They have fire in their mouths!"
"They'll kill us all!"
The mayor grabbed the town flag
and ran to the center of the square.
"Gather the biggest rocks you can find!
Defend yourselves!"

Nico left the town square
and walked down a quiet street.
He wondered what the enemy
really looked like.
The townspeople had never
seen the enemy.
That meant that the enemy had never
seen the townspeople, either.
Nico got a wonderful idea.
When the farmers brought their animals
inside the town walls,
Nico strode past them to get outside.
He went straight to the river
and sat on the bridge.
He shut his eyes and thought
of the saddest things he knew.
Soon Nico was crying.

Before long, the enemy army
marched up to the bridge.
"You, there. Who are you?"
called the captain.
"What are you doing there?"
Nico looked at the captain.
"They call me Nico," he said.
"And I'm here because no one likes me.
They make fun of me."
Nico stood up slowly.
The captain stared up at Nico.
He was afraid of giants,
even giants who cried.
But he smiled and tried to act brave.
"Of course everyone makes fun of you.
Just look at how strange you are."
The soldiers laughed.

"You're right," said Nico.

"I *am* different.

I'm the smallest one in town.

Everyone picks on me

because I'm always underfoot.

It's not fair!"

The soldiers scratched their legs.

They pulled their ears.

They tried to guess

how tall Nico really was.

The captain was quiet.

He was no coward.

On the other hand, he was no fool.

He turned around and shouted,

"Home, men!

We've won enough wars."

But the soldiers were already

running away.

The townspeople had been watching
Nico and the army
through peepholes in the walls.
They had been too afraid
to come outside.
As soon as the army disappeared,
they ran to the river to meet Nico.
They cheered and laughed.
They surrounded Nico,
and together they all marched
back to town.
Nico's mother and father
were very proud of him.
The mayor gave Nico a medal.

The townspeople built him a giant
house and gave him a new job
taking care of the small children.
Nico was happy for the rest of his life.

When Nico died,
the townspeople built a statue of him.
When the statue was finished,
the children of Barletta
began climbing on it.
They swung on it
and jumped from its arms.
They have been playing
on the statue ever since.